A Pocketful of Starlight

A Pocketful of Starlight

By Rubyha McKenzie
Illustrated by Denise Williams

First Edition
RMMP books may be purchased for educational, business, or sales promotional use through email contact:

rmohzie@outlook.com

Published by RRMP
Services by FriesenPress   ◆ FriesenPress
One Printers Way
Altona, MB R0G 0B0
Canada
www.friesenpress.com

1. *FICTION, FAIRY TALES, FOLK TALES, LEGENDS & MYTHOLOGY*

Distributed to the trade by The Ingram Book Company

Library of Canada Cataloguing in Publication

McKenzie, Rubyha *National*
A Pocketful of Starlight/ Rubyha McKenzie

ISBN
978-1-77815-940-4 (Hardcover)
978-1-77815-941-1 (Paperback)
978-1-77815-942-8 (eBook)

dedicated

to

the child in each of us...

Author: Rubyha McKenzie

Rubyha was born into a family of eight, of two very young parents. She grew up in a large extended family, in a home that still stands today, in San Fernando, Trinidad. Islamic by birth, she attended Anglican St. Paul's EC, Presbyterian Naparima Girls' High School, the University of Guyana, the AMI Institute in London, England, American University in Washington DC, the Washington Montessori Institute, and Loyola College: both in Baltimore MD, USA.

Interspersed with these educational pursuits, she was the wife of George Winston McKenzie, FSO of Trinidad & Tobago, mother to their twins Anya and David, and together, had the privilege of living in England, in the USA, and in Guyana, with a home base in Trinidad & Tobago.

Rubyha started off as a teacher in Trinidad at seventeen, and in every country in which she lived, including Canada, used her education and credentials to administrate, teach, or volunteer her skills, working with both children and parents, and with seniors, as a facilitator of creative writing. She has most recently completed the formation course of Catechesis of the Good Shepherd, for serving young children, utilizing the educational pedagogy of Dr. Maria Montessori.

Email: rmohzie@outlook.com

Illustrator: Denise Williams

"I believe my style to be detailed, and the love of colour is something that motivates my art. Also, that desire to capture nature untouched, or a piece of work in its most rugged, original form, for example, colonial buildings, is something that excites me.

I have always been in awe, and driven by, watercolour, possibly because of my early years seeing my mother do paintings of such - beach scenes and the world around her at that time, in watercolour. What I like most about it, is its simple effectiveness.

I had done art at school and had done quite well, but only in my adult years really stretched myself, fascinated by the work and style of local artists - Harry Bryden and Anthony Timothy.

Art for me presently extends also to oil, oil/chalk pastel, and in exploring sculpting. I am working hard in all these areas and plan to include abstract painting, as part of my portfolio." *Denise Edith Lenore Williams*

Email: dwilliams1301@gmail.com

The Stories   Pages

The Secret Life of the Flower Vendor

Each morning as the sun rose, Katya's cart was to be seen parked on the corner just across from Coronation Square. A wooden rickshaw filled with a riot of flowers—flowers of every colour and description. The early morning air, fresh and cool, punctured the senses with the scent of roses, lilacs, gardenia, and the musky smell of late autumn chrysanthemums. Katya herself was busy clipping stalks and organizing blooms into small bouquets for early morning commuters.

She was a diminutive woman of indeterminable age, crowned by a crescent of silver hair, under whose wispy bangs, large, steady, grey eyes gazed out with a hint of *je ne sais quoi*. Was it humour, cynicism, wit, drollery? No one seemed to know who Katya was, where she lived, or quite how she managed to eke out a livelihood from her flower sales. She had no ties to the community: she did not shop there, did not live there, and did not attend the local church. Come to think of it, no one actually saw her arriving at the street corner at six in the morning. She was just there, and there every morning, until that fateful morning in mid-December. No one remembered how long Katya's cart had actually occupied that corner. They just knew that on that cold December morning, it was not there. Katya's cart was never found.

But interestingly enough, around the same time of its disappearance, the local paper announced the death of a leading socialite, a woman, Dame Georgina Van Bruck. She had lived in the old manse just outside the village, with her faithful housekeeper, and her dog, Maxwell. Georgina herself had spent much of her time traveling, after being a leading light in the theatre.

The paper said she had played Portia in Shakespeare's *The Merchant of Venice*, and Miranda in *The Tempest*, as a young, aspiring actress. There was even talk of her playing Pygmalion in George Bernard Shaw's work of the same name. She had moved to the village some twenty years ago and spent her time travelling, giving lectures, and writing. Her one passion apart from the theatre, was her love for gardens and gardening. Dame Georgina had transformed the walled garden of the manse into a horticultural showpiece. No one ever suspected that behind those imposing walls lay a banquet for the senses. She laboured almost single-handedly every day for hours after lunch. She arose in the wee hours of the morning and drove her huge travelling van to the corner of Coronation Street. There, she rolled out the rickshaw of flowers, closed the van, and parked it underground. Her flowers gave joy to all who passed by, and no one was turned away for lack of change to pay for them. By twelve noon Katya had delivered the rest of the flowers to the nearby hospital, and rolled her rickshaw to the underground parking of the hospital. There she wheeled it into her parked van, removed her wig, uncoiled her long grey hair, and drove back to the manse. This she had done every day for the past fifteen years. Her gift to her world was her flowers.

The Little Shoe

Tully and I were taking an early morning walk in the park. The scent of wet soil was sending her bananas. Nose to the ground, tail aloft, she buried her muzzle in the soft, loamy winter detritus: decomposed leaves, stems, grass, flowers, and droppings. She pulled at the leash, and I had to run to keep up with her. The early morning sunshine spilled through the budding branches up above, and from time to time came the soft cooing of ground doves and the answering chirrups of airborne partners.

Lost in my own reverie, I did not realize that Tully had stopped pulling. She was focussed, and her tail quite still as she rooted feverishly in one spot. Finally dropping to her haunches, teeth embedded in some colourful material, she tugged from side to side. I watched in fascination as the object came free. It was a shoe of some kind. I had never seen a shoe like that before, though I had seen pictures of them, and read about them. It was still in pretty good shape, though covered in the loose winter loam of the coniferous forest. Tully dropped it at my feet, and I knelt to examine it. She looked at me, tail wagging, the corners of her mouth loose with satisfaction. It was a clog-type shoe. Its sides and top were gaily woven in colourful grass-like strips. Birds fluttered along its sides against a background of red, white, and pale blue. Across the front, black, green, and pink floral motifs boxed in the toes.

Around the aperture for the foot, ran a pale grey, beaded border. The sole for this small shoe was a solid wooden platform, lacquered in gold.

How beautiful! What could this exquisite little shoe be doing buried in the forest floor? Tully's brown eyes mirrored my curiosity. I pulled out one of her poo bags and tumbled the shoe into it, while Tully whined in perplexity. I patted her head and turned us around for home.

I went online and researched the shoe. Several pictures came up like it, except this found one, was more of a clog, without the laces or strap, and aperture not as small. I avidly read about it . . . Chinese . . . 1800s . . . used for binding girls' feet so that the growth remained stunted . . . maybe this shoe was not from China? Next, I looked up the demographics for my neighbourhood in the 1800s. Chinese, East Asians? Questions buzzed through my mind: Who were they? Did the shoe belong to a child or a young woman? Why was it in the forest? Where was the other side? Where did they live? Is that family alive today?

Yes, no doubt about it, there had been a wave of immigration in the 1800s . . . refugee boat people who had spread out and filtered into towns and villages looking for work. Would they have fled with this exquisite little shoe? It did not seem probable, but anything was possible. Maybe the child was attached to her shoe despite the torture it inflicted on her foot.

I cleaned up the shoe and placed it in a glass ornament box. It stands there, a question mark to the past but a catalyst for the future, as I methodically began to research the newspaper archives at the local library. This was the beginning of a new chapter in my life.

A Found Object

Palest pink washed the early morning skies. A silver crescent still hung low over the azure-peaked volcanic hills. Waves lapped gently along the beach, and schools of little fish swam in perfect unison, synchronized in their water ballet.

It was about five in the morning, and I was taking my early morning walk before starting the day's work. Toes scrunching, arms moving rhythmically to deep inhalations, each step firmly anchored in the wet sand, I treaded the beach at Grande Anse, Grenada, in the Caribbean. My eyes swept the horizon, noting the subtle changes as dawn slipped into morning. All along the beach, the low, squatting trees were laden with sea grapes, and mongrel dogs wagged their tails in hopeful greeting. I slowed my gait as the sand gave way to pebbly shale. As I looked down to carefully place my toes, I saw a glint of deep green. I stooped to examine it more closely and saw that it was translucent, flat and smooth. I picked it up and slipped it into my pocket. It would join the hundreds of found objects I kept in my patio basket.

As I walked home, my hand cupped the cool object in my pocket, feeling its smooth surface. How long had it taken for it to become so smooth? Where had it come from . . . from what land, beyond what sea? What made it cool and green? Could it have been a fragment of glass . . . maybe from a broken bottle thrown from some ship in bygone years? Where had that ship been heading? Maybe it was a rumrunner in Carib seas?

Later that day, after work, I took out my green talisman and examined it closely in the light. Sure enough, deep within its innards I could barely make out some sort of image. I got out my magnifying glass and peered into it. Yes, it was an image of some sort, but because it was buried deep within, I could not clearly access it. This would have to wait.

That summer I took it back with me to Canada and had it officially assessed by a maritime antique specialist. My beautiful green talisman turned out to be the remnants of a Norwegian fishing float, with an embedded PCF [1] seal at its bottom. I was shown a picture of what it would have looked like in its original form. It had been a beautiful green glass onion-shaped fishing float.

As I took my green talisman back home, I began to wonder about it. Who had it belonged to? A Norwegian fisherman? Why was it given a PCF marking? Why was this beautiful thing used for a fishing float? Were there many more like it? Well, here was more fodder for my very active mind . . . Norwegian fishing . . . and Norwegian fishermen . . . types of fishing floats . . . green glass . . . *Here we go again*, I thought.

Yes, it turned out to be my talisman indeed, for many years later, I connected with the family who made these fishing floats in the village of Bud, western Norway. And yes, that family was to join my own, but that is a story for another day.

---

1 +P.C.F.+ Old German Glass Fishing float with seal of initials at bottom; one source attributes initials PCF to Peter Christian Falchenberg who established a marine business in Norway in 1876

Let's Start from Scratch

Most famous starting words: "Let's start from scratch!"

The mother had been quietly responding to her mail, sitting at the table, while her youngest child sat on the floor beside her. He had been trying to build The Roman Arch.[2] He had sat on his knees. He had lain on his stomach. He had sat cross-legged and chewed his bottom lip. Each time he had built it up, and each time there was one block left.

Finally, he looked up at his mom. She stopped writing and looked silently at the plea in his eyes. "OK," she said. "Let's start from scratch."

She sat on the floor beside him and carefully sorted the blocks into groups of the same. There was only one block that did not belong to any group. That one stood alone. She held his eyes and slowly, carefully picked up one block, making sure that his eyes followed her movement, and placed it on the arch of the template. Their eyes met, and she picked up another. His eyes followed. In this way, without speaking, she placed all the blocks in place. There was one empty spot left. She paused and held his eyes for a split second longer, picked up the lone block and inserted it into position.

---

2 Montessori Roman Arch

Only then, before he could explode into sound, she quickly pulled the lever out from under the arch and watched his face as she withdrew the arch-shaped template that held the structure together. The arch of blocks held their shape and position.

He threw his arms around her neck. "I love you Mom," he said quietly.

He ran back to the arch and quickly unbuilt it, placing each block into a group of its own. He carefully placed the one that was left, in a spot all by itself. He looked up at his mom, their eyes met, and he continued on his own, without looking up again. If he had, he would have seen that she had gone back to answering her mail. Her mission was complete.

And so it has been, since the first human being used his hands as tools. From mud, bark, leaves, seeds, grain, berries, flowers, rock, wood, skins and pelts, bones and teeth, gut, ligament, hair and tendons, fire, metal, electricity, atomic energy, radioactive energy, nuclear energy, and information technology, he has abstracted their essence and stored their characteristics in his mind. Then he used these "essences" to create something he needed, to be able to survive in his environment. First the need arose, and he pondered on it. He imagined a solution and then went through his arsenal of materials around him. And each time a synaptic connection was made in his brain.

Step by step, starting from scratch many times over, he forged his own brain and his own consciousness by using his hands and his senses. Best words ever said: "Let's start from scratch."

Living to a Different Beat

The kids were grown and settled. She had worked all her life on contracts, bound to the letter of the law, and had been unable to pack her bags and head off into the wide blue yonder. Now was the right time. Her credit was good, and she finally had all her possessions under one roof.

Sabah had always wanted to go to the land of her ancestors, and so, recently, when she came across the BBC production done by Michael Woods, *The Story of India*, it had opened up a long-buried desire to know more. All she needed really was her credit card, her cell phone, her laptop, and camera—and of course sturdy walking shoes, a good UV protector, and a pair of cotton everything, including cargo pants with lots of pockets: wear one, wash one. Mentally she checked off her list, including a purse-size hand sanitizer, a good pair of sunshades on a lanyard, a collapsible umbrella, and - she would get the shot for Hepatitis A!

She booked her flight to New Delhi and splurged on a one-night stay at the Radisson Blue Marina Connaught Place. Once there, she had a wonderful breakfast, packed a doggie bag of filled parathas and Masala Bhujia: a sweet-savoury mix of nuts, split peas, and gram sticks with raisins, and bottled water. She checked out, hoisted her backpack, and, shod in her most comfortable sandals and her cotton things, set off for the train station.

Schedules and maps in hand, she stepped into the mêlée of humanity, eyes scanning and searching, nose twitching with the smells, and almost deafened by the indescribable sounds of this ancient civilization.

Sabah stopped at several guesthouses and B&Bs. She would look into the eyes of the proprietor, ask to use the washroom, and allow her gut to guide her. Smell was the most important currency here.

Finally, after about an hour's trek through the city, she found a small, quiet, clean guesthouse tucked away behind a wall draped with tangerine bougainvillea. There was a little kitchenette, a futon, and a table and chair. She examined the mattress carefully and then lowered her weary body onto the futon. Later, refreshed and cool, she went out to gather the vegetables, herbs, and grains she needed for food.

This was her base of operations. She spread out her maps, transit schedules, and guidebooks, and plotted her trips for the month. Next, she created a spreadsheet that was easy to access and calculated her costs, not forgetting to include the much-expected tips and gifts along the way. She would visit Uttar Pradesh, Haryana, The Punjab, and Uttarakhand. Next, she got out her guidebooks and listed all the sites she wanted to visit. This done, she got onto her laptop and researched these sites, getting the most up-to-date information and weather conditions. This was the start of another incarnation.

Freedom of Expression

They were a small group. They ranged in age from six to twelve, and they came from every walk of life.

There was Dino from Italy, and Eliza whose parents came from England. Jean was from Martinique, and Felipe from Uruguay. These latter two were both chatting with animation as they composed a palette of delightful colours. There were a few Canadians, some French-speaking, some not. Francois's parents worked with the ILO, and he spoke impeccable Parisian French. He was nine. Twelve-year-old Caroline was just visiting. Her parents were on a world cruise and had dropped anchor for a month. She was American. Vishnu came from India, and Bhagat, with his tightly wound turban, came from The Punjab. Mourid came from Palestine, and with the earnestness born of astute observation, he was busy sketching on his pad. There was little Alva, from Israel, barely six, busy with brush and pan, cleaning up the mess she had made with her early morning cereal. Obafemi wore the colours of his land in Africa. His little head was ensconced in an embroidered Kufi. He was also six. The little blonde girls, Ingrid and Athena, had one thing in common: they both loved to bake. Ingrid loved to bake Danish pastries, and Athena brought in phyllo dough to bake her baklava.

Every morning they gathered around in a circle to share their experiences. There was celebration of birth, and the passing of life. There was honour for the aged family members. Children spoke of their religious celebrations with their families, and of their holiday travels to distant homelands. There was love for pets and concern for trees, and lakes, and fish. They looked into each other's faces and saw mirrored there, their own emotions: joy, fear, pain, loneliness, sadness . . . and hope. They spoke of their lovely clothing, and what it meant to them. They also had the ritual of respectful silence while listening to each other's national anthems.

When it was time to choose their work, sometimes they chose to work alone, but most times, they paired up, or chose to work in groups, laughing and chatting as they planned how it would evolve.

In the midst of this happy hum of activity came a stifled sob. Obafemi was standing in front of the easel, tears streaming down his face. The children rushed over to have a look. There was the outline of a black cat wearing Obafemi's Kufi. Jean and Felipe looked at each other in consternation. What had they done? They were simply having fun, and Obafemi's hat was so colourful! They thought it would look great for Halloween! Stricken, they put down their brushes and hugged him while the other children all crowded around to comfort him. Jean and Felipe went back to the easel and quietly painted out the offending cat. The Kufi meant too much to Obafemi. Everyone watched, solemn-eyed, as the last smidgen of paint was covered and then they all went back to work.

The Man with the Gun

Haley pulled up the bedroom shutters and looked out. It was a gorgeous day. The early morning was still crisp and cool, but already the tinges of purple and pink were giving way to shimmering coral with streaks of fiery orange. After a long frigid winter, this was certainly a blessing.

One hour later she let herself into the garage through the kitchen entrance. In the half-light she opened the car door and slid into the driver's seat. She placed her cell phone on the seat within reach, adjusted the rear-view mirror, checked the wing mirror, and tumbled the ignition. As the car idled, she strapped herself into her seat belt, activated the garage door, and prepared to back out.

As she swivelled in her seat to look through the rear window, Haley uttered a piercing scream. There, on the back seat of her car, was a man, half-crouching, half-sprawled from seat to floor. He was holding a gun and waving it back and forth slowly, indicating that she should continue reversing. She looked at the gun and then at his face and inched the car backwards all the way to the road. Now she could see him in the rear-view mirror, still pointing the gun at the back of her head.

When she could, she would flip open the cell phone on the seat and press the fast call button . . . but for now she nosed the car along the street, exiting on Route 10 to Brampton. He started speaking. His name was Kereime. He was alone. It was too cold to walk.

He had lost his job, his family had not yet joined him, and he wanted someone to listen to his story. He had no money to travel, and had slipped into her car when she went in to carry her groceries last evening. The only person he knew lived in Brampton, and he had to get there. He had come to Canada a year ago in response to a job offer, and all had gone well until the company folded.

He had been given some compensation, but all of that was gone, and he had not been able to find another job. Haley wondered how many more were out there, just like him. There had been several reports of people found frozen to death in the cold. Kereime could have been one of them.

They rode in silence until she dropped him off at The Mission for Refugees. Haley found the gun on the floor of the car. It was a toy model.

Haley's life was never quite the same again. She became a volunteer at soup kitchens and worked for the homeless. Today, she is peace activist and works at the UN.

My Unicorn

The mists were rising even as the rosy hue of dawn tinged the clouds in palest pink. It had been a humid night, and I had not slept well, tossing and turning, wet with sweat. Finally, I slipped onto the cool floors, found my slippers, and crept outdoors.

The air was wet and cool. Every leaf was coated with a film of dew and created an incandescent haze in the early morning air. I picked my way carefully through the undergrowth around the house, fully aware of the myriad of tiny spores I was treading upon, breathing them into my lungs, and disturbing them, for I was the intruder. Except for the occasional crack of a twig, or crunch of leaves, silence cloaked the morning with a shawl of enchantment.

I left the house behind, and step by step took the path leading upwards. I could see the bare cliffs scarring the hillside and, from time to time, rivulets of water cascading down onto the canopy below. Where this happened, mists formed and rose upwards, capturing fractured light. I stood spellbound, watching the spill of indescribable colour bathing the craggy hilltops. As I became enveloped in this splendid show, I saw a form that I could not believe was real. I shut my eyes and opened them again. It was still there. I rubbed them and carefully opened them again. There she was. I thought instinctively that she must be female. She was slender and stood tall, legs long and fawn-like, head perfectly still.

Even from a distance I could tell that her eyes were like pools of blue light. She was shimmering white, and the one horn in the middle of her head was at least eighteen inches long. What a beautiful horn! White from base to midpoint, and at its tapering end a braid of many colours. I had read of it, but never believed that it existed. This creature of fantasy and myth right here before my very eyes.

I leaned against a tree for support, never taking my eyes from this vision, until I slipped to the ground, finding myself sprawled in a pile of dried vegetation. It was cool and comfortable here, and my unicorn was still looking down upon me. Where had she come from? Was she just a vision conjured up by mist and sunlight? Was she a spirit guide come to give me a message? I thought of my mom who had passed on . . . where was she? Suddenly the chasm that separated us was no more. I knew for sure that if this mythical creature could be conjured up out of nowhere, then my mom was also somewhere waiting . . . maybe that was why this beautiful creature had come to me in the morning mist.

I closed my eyes, not afraid to let this creature go. She had done her work, and I had found peace. I turned on my side, and tucking my arms under my head, I fell asleep.

The Binoculars

I was made of red leather, chrome, and glass. I was collapsible and compact. When open, I was two inches wide at the lens, and about one inch across at the back, where human eyes peered through me.

I had lived for many a year in a glass case in a shop in Soho, London and spent many a lively morning being peered into, by blue, grey, brown, black, and even green eyes, off and on. People would hold me up to their eyes and peer out into the streets, up into the sky, across at the apartment buildings and I would have a chance to see what the world looked like. I particularly loved the green of trees . . . and sometimes I would see birds nesting in trees. I hated trains because, if the person did not turn their head fast enough, the train would disappear from view.

One day, a woman in her late fifties came into the shop and picked me up gently. I knew just by the way she held me, that this was a caring person. She did not put me to her eyes right away, but cleaned my lens, adjusted the nose width, rubbed the dark red leather and the chrome till they shone, and then held me to her eyes. Her irises were black, and she had long eyelashes. She paid for me and had me gift-wrapped.

That weekend there was a birthday party for her niece, Rosamunde, and I was lovingly presented in a gift bag.

The young girl pulled the ribbon, opened the box, and carefully lifted me out. She turned to her aunt and flung her arms around her. "How did you know that I wanted these?" she asked.

Her aunt simply reached over and held out the gift bag to her. There, nestled inside the bag were tickets to see Verdi's opera, *Nabucco*.[3] She had always wanted to see *Nabucco* on stage, and her aunt had remembered and bought her the tickets and the opera lens! This time Rosamunde lost no time. She opened the lens, put them to her eyes, and twirled around the room singing with delight.

Rosamunde and her aunt attended *Nabucco* later that month. It was the beginning of a wonderful relationship, with me tucked into her tiny evening bag. I kept company there with a folded tissue for cleaning my lenses. I learned a lot about the Hebrews and Nebuchadnezzar, and enjoyed the powerful *Prisoner's Chorus*.

Well, that's the end of my story. Rosamunde's story continued as she grew up and attended many an opera, sometimes alone, when I kept her company and learned many a musical score. Most times she went with a young gentleman, and then I was always forgotten, as her head invariably rested on his shoulder throughout the performance, and I stayed in her purse. Now, Rosamunde has passed away, and I have been boxed and placed in a drawer, waiting for another pair of gentle, caring hands.

---

3 *Nabucco*: opera by Giuseppe Verdi

A Stolen Ring

She gave it to me when last I saw her. It was made of a heavy, silver metal, and its thick, round, pewter crown held within its core a clear, light blue, Celestine-like stone. This faceted stone was riveted to the centre by five tiny metal claws, and around its pale blue light, six petal-like flaps exploded away to the perimeter of the crown. It was magical. I hefted it in my palm and liked the feel of it. She said it was a gift from her to me.

It was my favourite ring, and whenever I wore it, she was with me. Long after she had passed on, that ring fascinated me. One night as I sat twirling it in my fingers, I noticed that there was very fine text on the inside of the band. I could not read it with the naked eye, so I got a magnifying glass and focused it so that I was able to discern the small, capitalized letters: ABC 3 905 Mexico. My heart started to beat faster. What could that mean?

She had travelled extensively in her youth, pursuing her dream of being a nurse. Could it have been given to her by a grateful patient? Could she have bought it in some exotic bazaar? It looked like something a fortune-teller would wear.

Many months later, as I worked the floor at a reception, I looked up to see a pair of laughing, black eyes staring at my hands intently. I followed his gaze to the ring on my finger.

He said, "Can we speak privately?"

Of course, I had no intention of having a tête-á- tête with a complete stranger, so I said, "Certainly. Let me get my husband."

I half-expected him to disappear, but he just stood and waited.

We drifted out onto the patio, and there he introduced himself as a member of the Barajas family. He apologized for staring at my ring, and said that the design of the ring was very significant to his family. He wanted to know its history. I told him about my friend who had gifted me with this ring. He insisted on knowing her name and so I shared my story with Señor Barajas.

To my amazement, when I was finished, he pulled out from his pocket an identical ring on a chain. He said he was one of a set of twins, and at birth, both he and his sister were given identical rings by their great-grandfather, Alonso. His twin sister had died many years ago in England, and of course, no trace of the ring had ever been found until now. His eyes filled with tears as he spoke of his sister. The family thought maybe someone had stolen the ring.

And then I remembered that my friend had worked at The Charing Cross Hospital in London many years ago. I asked Señor Barajas where his sister had died. He confirmed that she had passed away at a hospital near the Charing Cross railway station. I shared my information with him, and he grew silent. He did remember his sister writing about a nurse who took care of her. As I looked at him, I felt his pain for his beloved sister. I was about to offer him the ring when he said, "My sister brought you to me, so that I would have peace and resolution. I know the ring is safe and was given in love. She would want you to keep it. But you must promise to take care of it and to pass it on only with love. To do otherwise would only bring misfortune on that person."

Señor Barajas left then, but I never forgot his words. I still have the ring.

That Tapping is Not the Steam Heat, is it?

Miranda had completed her work in the kitchen. She checked all the burners to make sure that they were off. The kettle was unplugged, the fridge door was firmly closed, the faucet was properly turned off, and the floor had been mopped. She left the TV on The National while she performed her nightly ablutions, applied face cream, brushed her hair, and anchored it in a loose knot on the top of her head. She switched off the TV and climbed into bed. She read a bit from *Anil's Ghost*[4] before reaching for the lamp's chain. Then she remembered: she had not checked the front door.

Now, Miranda did not have a safety chain on her door. Instead, she pulled up the long, heavy rubber matting against the door rolling her trolley against its base, turning it sideways so that the wheels could not roll. Only then could she fall asleep.

And sleep she did. She was sure it was about two in the morning when she was awoken by a sound. At first there was this faint tap at regular intervals, insistent in her sleep-drugged mind . . . tap-tapping slowly until she could bear it no more. She lifted her head off the pillow. Now she could hear it clearly. She flipped open her cell phone and looked at the time. It was not yet three.

---

4 *Anil's Ghost*, novel by Michael Ondaatje

Miranda sat up, slipped on her slippers, found the flashlight under her bed head, and went into the darkened hallway. She stared at the door. As she watched, she saw the handle turning.

Someone was outside, turning the door handle. A scream rose in her throat, but she quickly stuffed her fist into her mouth. She must think.

There was the tap-tapping again. They were trying to spring the lock! She dialled for help, 999 on her cell, and began to quietly pile every heavy thing she could think of into the trolley: her weights, her tool kit, her bag of rocks . . .

Ten minutes later, she heard a firm rap at the door and, "Ma'am. It's the police. You can open the door now."

Miranda said, "Call me on my phone."

Her phone rang and she picked it up.

"This is Officer Ryan. We are at your door. You are safe. Please open the door."

Miranda leaned down and dragged the heavy matting and trolley away from the door. She opened the door and stepped out. There was no floor. No hallway. She fell like a stone, down, down, down, the wind rushing past her as the air in her lungs ricocheted in a piercing scream . . .

A cool tongue was slowly lathering her face with wet, sloppy licks, and a cold, wet nose pushed against her throat, whining softly. Miranda opened her eyes, blinking in the strong sunlight streaming through her bedroom window. Bella's golden-brown eyes peered into her face. She had one paw on Miranda's chest, the other behind her head on the pillow. Slowly, Miranda lifted her arms and hugged this wonderful friend. Thank God, it had all been a dream!

Broderick

He was long, lithe, black, and beautiful. Nine out of ten times he was sound asleep. You wondered what he did to make himself so tired. Well, truth be told, he was not really asleep. If you looked closely enough, you would see those slit-eyes were not quite tightly shut. Yes, he was curled up into a ball, and the even rise and fall of his chest would have fooled even the most astute observer. Broderick had a secret, a passion. He was a thief.

As soon as he was alone, he sprang into action. His long silky tail took on a life of its own. It curled upwards and its tip darted around like a snake. Yellow eyes fully open, he made the rounds. Nana's room was on the ground floor, and she was in the shower. Her beautiful, jewelled hair combs were scattered on the bed. Pearls and opals reflected quietly among the bed sheets. He had to work quickly before she returned. Broderick leaped onto the bed and, baring his teeth, clamped down firmly on a comb. He could hear Nana coming down the stairs. He bolted under the bed and remained there until she left to pick up the children. Only then did he scurry down into the basement.

When Nana and the children returned, Broderick was firmly ensconced in his basket near the fire. They took turns stroking his soft fur, and his eyes fluttered in ecstasy. Mother was setting tea out in the garden, and the children changed and went out to play.

Nana was in her room shaking out the bed sheets. She was missing her hair comb and was almost distraught with anxiety. It was very special, and it was not the first time she had misplaced something beautiful and valuable. Last spring, she had been sitting on the front porch enjoying her evening cuppa. She had taken off her lapis ring and laying it on the magazine she had been reading, she had gone to the washroom. She had forgotten all about it until later that night. With flashlight in hand, she had gone out to the porch looking all over. She even went to the washroom. Maybe it had gone down into the plumbing? She did not dare tell the family. With her poor hearing and even poorer eyesight, this would be just one more thing that would be chalked up to her aging sensibilities. She had resolved then to say nothing about it, hoping that it would turn up; and now, her best hair comb was missing! Nana was spooked.

She left her room wearily and was about to sit in the family room when she observed that Broderick was not in his basket, and not on the ground floor level. She wondered where he had gone to as she settled into her armchair. She had almost dozed off when she heard the distinct *ping* of something falling. Everyone was outside in the garden . . . only she and Broderick were indoors, and he had disappeared. Was he upstairs? What was he doing? Slowly, with eyes closed, she turned her head toward the stairs. What she saw, she would never have believed in her wildest dreams. Broderick was creeping down the stairs, and he was carrying Alice's sequined Halloween slipper! He headed straight down to the basement.

That evening, Nana organized a treasure hunt in the basement. She planted written clues in every nook and cranny, so that the children would eventually scour out the entire area—rafters and all!

It was almost midnight when they came screaming into her room. "Nana, look what we found . . . all these things that were missing . . . and Nana, here is your ring and your comb! Did you put them there?"

Nana smiled softly and said, "I must have been sleepwalking!"

Geschenk Vom Eis

Once upon a time, in a land of mountains, forests, woodlands, and vast wastelands, there lived a king and his beautiful queen. They had two children who were the pride and joy of their lives. The boy was called Yacob, and the girl Wilhelmina.

These children loved the snow and ice and would spend their days skating over the frozen ponds, lakes, and wastelands. The king and queen would become very anxious about them, but never prohibited them from skating. They just wished they would not go so far away, or skate in the early spring or winter when the ice was melting, and dangerous.

Yacob and Wilhelmina loved their parents and tried very hard not to cause them too much anxiety: they only skated in the dead of a very frozen winter. One day however, they were just out playing in the snow when they heard a cry for help. It came from a small wooded area. They quickly set off to find its source. There, in the middle of the barren trees, was a small pond. They could see a crack in the ice, and a hole. Suddenly, a hand poked out of the hole, flailing wildly. Both children almost leapt onto the ice, but stopped short as they remembered the promise to their parents. They looked at each other in desperation.

They both could not go onto the ice . . . but maybe one could go carefully, if doing a belly-crawl. Wilhelmina was smaller and lighter. She would do the crawling, but he had to find a way to anchor her, just in case. Yacob looked around for something to wrap around his sister's waist. He pulled off his scarf, and hers too, and tied them together. Then he tied one end around Wilhelmina's waist and the other to the stump of a nearby tree. After they double-checked all the knots, Wilhelmina crept to the hole on her stomach, as far as possible from the crack. She used her gloved hand to stir the water and shouted, "Halloooo!"

She repeated this a few more times and waited. She was about to shout again when she saw the faint flutter of a hand! She flicked the water again, and the hand came up. She grasped it . . . but her hand was getting too cold. Quickly, she flung off her hat and shook out her long braids. One fell into the water, and she guided the frozen hand to grab hold of it. From the tree stump, Yacob watched anxiously. He would go for help, but he could not leave her.

Suddenly, out of the corner of his eye, he saw movement above. Birds. Huge and black. He had never seen eagles that large. As he watched them grow closer, they formed into a ladder descending down to the pond. The one nearest to Wilhelmina latched its long talons around her frozen wrist. The ladder backed up and up. The mighty birds flapped their wings and rose higher, and her head and shoulders emerged from the water.

Wilhelmina screamed, "Don't let go! Hold on, you are almost out!"

Higher and higher they rose, all seven birds, and the little girl rose up out of the pond. She was a dead weight with her sodden clothes and boots, but they lifted her up and over the pond while Wilhelmina crept backwards to the edge. Yacob was there to help her out, and they both stood and watched the birds. They flew higher and higher until they disappeared.

Many years later, in the spring, when the land was covered with heather and bluebells, and the air was scented and soft, the young prince Yacob set out on horseback to explore the kingdom. His father, the king, was ailing, his mother, the queen, had died, and Wilhelmina had taken on the queen's duties at the palace. After many days of travel, Yacob came upon a wooded area and stopped to rest. He heard voices singing softly and followed them.

There, in the thicket, lying in a glass coffin, was a beautiful girl. Seven shrivelled old men were slowly walking around this coffin, singing mournfully in rich harmony. Yacob did not want to scare them, so he joined the circle too, humming low and deeply.

When they stopped, he introduced himself and enquired politely who she was. They told him a story of a frozen girl they had found on a pond many years ago. They had called her, *Eisjungfrau*, the frozen maiden. She had never awoken, but neither had she died. They had taken care of her all these years, waiting for her to wake up. Yacob went up to the coffin and opened it. Bending his knee, he took the hand of the sleeping girl, and kissed it. The cold hands became warm while he held them. Her bosom began to heave gently, and her eyes fluttered open. They were the most beautiful eyes he had ever seen. The seven men clustered around in joy, and that day was a day of celebration, a day of dancing and singing, rivalled only by the day when the young prince took her to be his wife.

The strangest part of the story was that when Eisjungfrau became pregnant and craved rampion[5], it was Wilhelmina who carried the baby. And the baby grew into the most enchanting girl, with Eisjungfrau's beautiful eyes, and Wilhelmina's long, golden tresses. They called this baby *Geschenk Vom Eis*—gift from the ice! She became the empress, and her reign was a golden one.

Note: This story was inspired by the stories of *Rapunzel recorded by* The Brothers Grimm *(1812)* and of *Schneewittchen (Snow White and the Seven Dwarfs),* revised in 1854 by The Brothers Grimm.

---

5 Campanula rapunculus, a plant whose leaves and root are edible. The tale of *Rapunzel* by the Brothers Grimm took its name from this plant.

Black as Pitch

Black as pitch, softer than night, I could hear the sound of waves crashing on sand, and the keening of the wind as it caressed the long, swishing, palm fronds. Unforgettable.

I was lying in the warm, shallow, riverbed far inside the entrance of the cave. Thermal underground springs fed into the stream much higher up, and the natural minerals in the water lit up like fireflies from time to time. Dreamily, I closed my eyes and allowed my head to rest in the bubbling, quiescent broth.

My fingers dug into the silty mush, and my toes frolicked along the sand bar. I could feel the fluted edges of the scallops and the coiled tops of the nautilus. My toes continued to play, digging and probing . . . how on earth did they get here? Surely they needed the salt water to survive? Maybe once upon a time there was no cave here. Maybe the ocean covered this space. How long ago was that? How did the caves get formed? Volcanic activity? That would account for the thermal springs. My eyes fluttered open, and I searched the velvety darkness above. Only the chirps and squeaks of bats as they sailed far above: *what would they find to eat in this cave?*

As I listened, another sound, much nearer, filtered into my consciousness, and before I could flip over to check it out, I had company. A soft gurgling whistle erupted near my ear, and I spluttered to a stop. The metallic, slightly salty water filled my mouth while I thrashed out with arms and legs, trying to fend off my invisible companion.

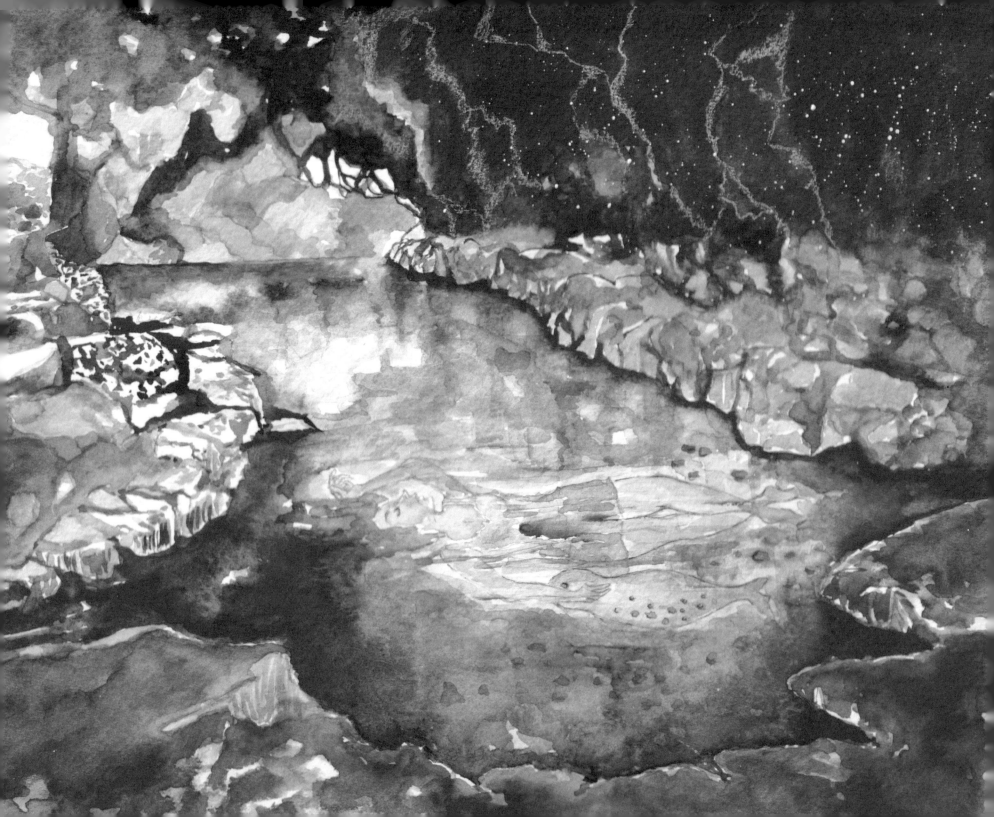

It whistled again, much higher and clearer. Was this creature trying to say something to me? Gingerly, I put my hand out and felt a smooth, soft outline. I ran my fingers along its length. It was about three feet long, and it remained perfectly still. A porpoise? Here? Its body was stout and its head was bulbous. There were no arms or fins. Then there was a series of whistles and a gurgle as it slipped away into the darkness. I felt that I had made a friend.

I do not know how long I remained there. I must have drowsed in the warm, tangy water. All the aches and pains of yesterday's climb had washed away. I could hear the gulls screeching in the early morning. No light had as yet filtered into the cave. I climbed out of the water, slipping and sliding as I pulled at the weeds and rocks near its edge. It was warm, so I pulled off my clothes and wrung them out. Bending down, I felt grass around my feet. I spread them out to dry, and lay down right beside them.

That's where the search party found me. My eyes flickered open, and I blinked in the bright light. Someone was holding a flashlight in my face. I quickly grabbed my clothes, shielding my nakedness. Gentle hands helped me dress and lifted me to my feet. They guided me to a waiting boat and pushed off in the darkness. Much later I could see a tiny opening in the distance. Daylight beckoned.

Do You Believe in Angels?

Cassandra put down the bag of groceries and fished in her pocket for her key. As she had done umpteen times before, she inserted the key into the lock, turned it and let herself in quietly. A whiff of something familiar hit her nostrils, and then it was gone.

Tama and Ronin uncurled themselves from the sofa and hump-backed their way over to her, unfurling their tails like majestic cobras. As she scratched under their chins, her nostrils quivered again. There was that smell again. What was it? She knew it, but it remained just beyond the reach of her conscious mind.

Shoes in one hand, she padded her way into the kitchen, reaching on the counter for her favourite green mug. It was not there. Strange, she always left it there. She opened the dishwasher to get a glass, and there was her green mug. *Hmm* . . . She set her shoes down on the tray and looked around for her slippers. They were not on the tray where she had left them. How irritating. Her feet were cold walking on the bare floor. Maybe she was getting potty . . . what had she done with them?

Tired from her shopping, she climbed into her favourite chair, reached for a magazine, and pulled the blanket over her legs. She would find those slippers later. Tama and Ronin snuggled down beside her feet, and she drifted off.

Between sleep and wake, Cassie's mind wrestled with that scent . . . and her mug . . . and her slippers. Something was not right. Someone was tidying up after her. Who on earth could it be? Someone had to have the key to her home. Had she ever given it to anyone else? She had been living here alone since Peter passed away twenty years ago. Peter? Her mind drifted to those bygone years and those last days . . . She had been so overcome with grief, and people had been so kind. How had she made it through she would never know . . . There was Hannah, and her husband Cole. Was there someone else? She struggled for a name . . . Nat . . . Nathan . . . And then it came back slowly. Nathaniel . . . *Oh my gosh!* Where was he now? He had slipped away out of her life right after the funeral. He was Peter's youngest brother, barely out of his teens then. He used to come in to help her when she could not even remember what day it was. He brought in groceries and fed the cats. Little by little, the pieces came together. She must have given him a key.

Cassie opened her eyes and reached for her bag. She found Nathaniel's phone number, and with trembling fingers dialled it. A deep voice answered: "Nathan here."

She responded, "Cassandra here. When are you coming over? You can let yourself in for dinner. It's fish and chips tonight—I know that's your favourite!"

He did not miss a beat. He came right over, letting himself in.

The cats curled up on his lap while he puffed away at his pipe. As Cassie's eyes met his over the cloud of tobacco smoke, she knew that he had always been there watching over her as the years passed. He had been her Angel.

The Shoe of Northumberland

She had been gone for almost six hours. They thought she would never come back.

"Ma is coming! Ma is coming!" Sigourney's high-pitched voice trilled through the cavernous forest. As quick as lightning, all seventeen children dropped from branches, scurried from under bushes and from behind rocks. Every man jack found his task.

Daisy and Emma had been making daisy chains to garland the windows of their home for spring. Aldrich and Beasley got back to milking the goat, which was tied to the old birch tree. Aelfric and Edith, the oldest of the lot, had been set the task of stirring the huge pot of vegetable broth. Tiny twins, Ava and Isabella, were busy removing twigs and dried leaves from an apron filled with berries. Rhoslyn and Margery, blonde and golden, were churning the cream to make butter. Two older boys, Arundel and Baul, had been chopping wood to start a fire. The other five children had been pulling up roots to find vegetables. Barric and Trea swung a basket of mushrooms while Achard and Heloise dragged a bag of wild roots of all colours. Little Gisella had been busy plucking wild thyme, mint, sage, and green onions.

Everyone was busy as Dame Gretchen emerged from the forest. She was riding side-saddle on her gryphon. Aylwin bent his knees, and she slipped to the ground. So many children . . . her eyes skimmed the crowded forest floor.

The sun's rays were lengthening. It was getting late. She could see their home casting a giant shadow in the distance. It was the magical shoe left to her by the Giant of Northumberland. She could never run out of space. It was that knowledge that had led her to take in these children.

She stuck two fingers into her lips and whistled hard. The children gathered around her. She scanned their anxious faces. She had been so upset with them when she left. These poor urchins had known only abuse, loneliness, and poverty. They had almost driven her to desperation. She had toiled, showing them how to cook and clean, how to be kind to each other, how to plant seeds and forage for food, but they had been mean and lazy. They had preferred to play all day and let her do the work. Finally, in disgust she had given them some broth without any bread, scolded them, whipped their hands, and sent them to bed.

She had left early that morning, flying off in the dawn's light, not knowing what was the solution. Now, as she looked at their expectant faces, she saw that her labour had not been in vain. She fetched the whip, broke it, and threw it into the fire under the cauldron of soup. The children cheered and rushed forward to hug her. They had tasted of the fruits of freedom, discipline, and responsibility, and she knew that they would never be the same again. They had found true freedom. As the sun sank into the western horizon, they had their dinner out of doors, and then tiredly but happily they all trooped into their home-The Shoe of Northumberland!

Note: This story was inspired by, *There was an Old Woman Who Lived in a Shoe*, published in 1794, of unknown origin

The Wrong Turn

Jody remembered exactly where she was supposed to turn left. There was a lovely old birch tree right at the corner. She did as she remembered, but after walking for a few minutes she realized that nothing was familiar. The track petered out into the woods, and instead of the familiar sight of the river on one side, there was a low escarpment in the distance.

A prickle of fear ran along her spine. Where was she? She looked up, and the sun was right overhead. She had been walking for about one hour now. The escarpment was too far away. She would head into the woods, and hope she made it through before late evening.

As she walked, she lost all perspective of time. Gnats buzzed in her ear, and leaves crunched underfoot. Silence echoed around her. The darkened tree trunks rose majestically, but she plodded on, vaguely conscious of her throbbing limbs and the coil of hunger deep in the pit of her stomach. She would not give it her energy. She would focus on finding something, someone, anything . . . She closed her eyes briefly and saw her mother's face. Her eyes flew open as she heard them. She could not see them, but far above the canopy, the Canada geese were honking their way south. Jody felt comforted. She could visualize them in formation, sailing on the wind.

A twig cracked nearby, and Jody turned in its direction. A deer was standing perfectly still, looking directly at her. She moved in its direction, and it bounded away to the right. Jody followed, and there before her stood a house.

It was magnificent. Light poured out of every window, and flares in tall sconces lined the walkways and turrets. It seemed familiar. The deer had disappeared. She approached the front door and turned the aging handle. To her surprise, it opened easily. She entered an enormous foyer lit by a low-hanging chandelier. Stairways branched up to the left and right. Jody entered and walked from room to room, each more ornate than the other. Everything was in a state of readiness, except there was not a single person, dead or alive.

Jody helped herself to water and nuts and then curled up on the sofa, pulled a rug over her legs, and fell fast asleep.

She awoke to the sound of voices and of wheels rolling.

"Hey! Over here! There is a girl!"

Jody sat up and looked around. A huge spotlight was on her face.

Someone said, "Turn off the lights!"

She could see them all now. It was a camera crew, and they were filming. People were in costume. She was in the middle of a movie set. Jody remembered where she had seen this house now. It had been featured in *Town and Country*, and it was on the other side of the river. She had taken the wrong path, way before the birch tree.

An Unwritten Code

We heard the approaching horses and hurried further into the woods. I grasped Madeleine's hands. They were cold and clammy. "Shush," I said, for she had begun to whimper. "It's OK," I whispered. "Just up ahead . . ." I did not finish that last sentence. A flight of black crows fled for cover at our approach. I looked up into the fading evening light and said a prayer. Madeleine was just a child, and she was badly scared. I would have to take care of her.

I looked at her closely. Her face was tear-streaked and wan. Her pinafore was torn and stained with the juice of berries that we had been foraging. We were both hungry and tired. I thought of what my father would do. People who hunted and lived in the forest had an unwritten code. Parcels of food were sometimes left in strategic places. By now we were deep into the forest, and could hear the sound of water. Sure enough, as we turned the corner around the huge banyan tree, there was a pool of water with a small stream feeding into it. I cupped my hands into a bowl and drank deeply from the stream and Madeleine followed suit. As she drank, my eyes roved. And then I saw it. Just in the bank of the stream there was a small ledge. Sitting on the ledge was a clay pot. I waded into the water and headed for it. Grasping with both arms, I carried it over to a clearing on the forest floor. The stopper was tightly wadded with dried lichen. I used a sharp stick to pry it open and turned it over onto the ground. Small, tightly-wrapped leather bundles fell out. I began to open them one by one.

There was smoked fish and dried sausage. Another one had a round of hard cheese. There were raisins and dried fruit, and finally, some small flat oatmeal biscuits. It was truly a feast for weary travelers.

I held Madeleine's hands, and together we gave thanks for food, and for the hands that had prepared and stored it. I did not have much, but I took off my amulet and put it into the pot, restored the lid, and put the pot back on the ledge.

Night had fallen, and come what may, we had to sleep. I leaned against a wide tree trunk for support and Madeleine snuggled into my lap. I used my cape to cover us both, and without another thought we drifted off to sleep. It must have been the wee hours of the morning when, stiff with cold and aching, I awoke to the sound of hoofbeats. Someone was riding hard. The events of the past two days flashed before my eyes: the horror of the raid on our hamlet; pillaging marauders setting fire to the barns and crucks; the smell of burning horse flesh, the terrorized whinnying, and the blind bolting . . .

Madeleine began to stir. I quickly placed my fingers against her lips to stifle her yawn. She had seen her parents caught in the fire, and it was at that point that I had dragged her away.

We were alone, she and I . . . and the rider.

The Fringes of Time

Omari snuggled down into the folds of canvas. They had been travelling through the night, and he was cramped and cold. But sleep would not come. Wearily, he threw off the canvas and sat up. There was a faint glimmering in the eastern sky.

As he watched, shades of pearly pink dappled with amethyst threaded the morning horizon. How skilfully Allah wove the colours just right for his early morning eyes! They were headed for Agadez, but that was days away.

Looking up, he saw a faint glimmer. They had arrived at the only watering hole before their journey's end in two days. Someone had left the remnants of a fire, deeply banked. Taj unhooked the animals and led them to drink. The women huddled around the pit, blowing hard to revive the coals. Soon chai would be ready, and they would break naan.

He wandered off. In the early morning light, everything was luminescent. Sand surrounded him. Sand banked, sand loose: each crease the wings of a bird. Not wings . . . letters. He began to spell out the letters as he read aloud slowly . . .

Prayer is not asking.

It is the longing of the Soul.

It is a daily admission of one's weakness.

It is better in prayer to have a Heart without Words

than Words without a Heart.[6]

Omari rubbed his eyes in disbelief . . .

It was still there. He had learned those words from his ancestor, the Sheik Ibn Akbar. It was his family's prayer, written in the tabeej[7] around his neck.

He began to cry softly, and, as he watched, the wind gently erased each letter from the sand. He turned around and headed back to the fire to have chai and naan.

---

6 Attributed to Mahatma Gandhi, whose *Book of Prayers* include 108 passages from Hindu and Moslem literature.

7 Tabeej or ta'wiz is an amulet or locket worn by some Muslims for good luck and protection from evil. Thy contain qur'anic verses and/or other Islamic prayers.

"Prayer is not asking.
It is the longing
of the soul.

It is a daily admission
of one's weakness

It is better in prayer to
have a heart without words

Than words without
A heart"

First Solo Flight

It was a crisp, cool morning. The sky was periwinkle blue and cloudless. In the distance he could see the Northern Range still shrouded in early morning mist. As he walked toward the small Piper Cub, the sound of the crunching gravel beneath his feet felt good. He had waited so long for this moment.

Rickey Fitzgibbon had finally completed his pilot training. The long months of gruelling training were finally over. How many times had he walked this way to take the Piper out? Rickey had ceased to count. His co-pilot and trainer had watched him with pride yesterday as he graduated with his "wings." Jacob was a stern taskmaster, but out of respect, friendship was born. Today, for the first time, he would fly without Jacob. It was his first solo flight.

The Piper Cub was ready and waiting on the tarmac. She was all aluminum grey and blue, backlit by dawn's light. Rickey climbed on board and checked the controls. The engine chugged to life. He powered the radio. The transmission came to life, and he requested clearance. Clearance was given. His moment had arrived. The Piper nosed forward along the tarmac and began to build speed. He had done this hundreds of times. As he turned onto the runway, all engines roared into life, and he sped away, building speed until there was lift off . . . a feeling like no other: he was a bird. This was why he had learned to fly. Everything else was secondary.

Rickey was set to cross the Northern Range, and the plane climbed effortlessly. He would have to take her up to forty thousand feet before levelling out on the other side. It was a clear, calm day, with the best possible flying conditions. Within five minutes he had cleared the range, and he could see the Caribbean Sea spread out way below. Then he picked up a slight hesitation on the descent. He planned to level out at thirty-five thousand feet, but she was not slowing down. His glance at the control panel confirmed his worst fears; the needles were going crazy. The expanse of blue water was coming up fast.

Breathe! he coached himself. *You are trained to handle this . . . what are your options? Send out a distress signal? Bail out?* He would lose the plane. He looked at the controls again and glanced at the panel above with the model number of his plane. It was a Piper Cub, but it was a PA 18 Super Cub. He could hardly believe it! It was fitted with floats. Rickey prepared to engage the floats as he approached the water. There was a flashing sign now: **DEPLOY**. He hit the button.

Unbelievable—from one second of mind-numbing fear to a soft, cushiony landing. He was afloat. Had Jacob arranged for the PA 18 Super Cub to be on the landing?

One hour later, the coast guard found him. The Piper was intact, and he had completed his first solo flight.

The Frog and The Princess

It was a windy fall day, and Horatio the Frog watched the last leaves flutter from the almost-naked birch trees.

Soon he would have to make up his mind to dive to the bottom of the pond and remain there for the winter months. It had been many years now since he had first been condemned to this eternal wetness, and he longed to be set free. He had waited and waited for a beautiful, young princess to come along, but winter had come and gone, and she never came.

He sighed deeply and was about to slip back into the water when he heard the sound of running footsteps. As he peered out from under his heavy lids, a young woman ran into the court yard. He had seen her many times before but always dove into the pond at her approach. She was not his beautiful princess. She was the king's daughter yes, but she was ugly. The king had refused to marry King Olaf's daughter, and a spell had been cast upon his first-born Princess Alia. She was born with bulbous eyes and . . . come to think of it, she resembled him, Horatio, a bit!

Today she was weeping bitterly, and Horatio forgot his own troubles as he lifted his head to listen better.

The princess sobbed out her story to her woodland playmates. The king her father was very ill. He needed some herbs that grew at the bottom of the pond, and there was no way that she could bring them up.

Horatio listened carefully and then dove deep into the murky depths of the pond.

Sure enough, there were rhizomes buried in the muddy bottom. He uprooted a large bulb and dragged it up to the surface.

With a flying leap, he dropped it at her feet and with a deep croak said, "My Princess, this is for your father!"

"Yes! That is the water hawthorn!" she said. "Thank God, you found it! Now my father will not die."

Princess Alia almost sped away but caught herself in time . . .

"I must thank you. What is your name?"

"Horatio, at your service ma'am."

"Can I give you a kiss?" she asked.

Horatio blushed to the bottoms of his webbed feet, thinking to himself, *Do I really want this? I cannot let her kiss me. She is so ugly!* He looked into her bulbous blue eyes, and saw all the kindness of her soul. He could not refuse her. Closing his eyes, he said, "Princess! Please do!"

Alia got down on her knees, and kissed Horatio's damp head.

Horatio felt as if he had been hit by a bolt of lightning! His heart pounded, his brain spun around, and he fell into a deep sleep. When he awoke, it was to find a beautiful Alia and the restored king looking down at him. He was in a huge bed hung with fine canopies of rich velvet.

Horatio and Alia gazed at each other. She held his hand and drew him to stand beside her. He no longer had webbed feet and wet green skin. Her lips were well-formed, and beautiful, blue eyes looked at him with adoration.

"Ahem," said the king, clearing his throat. "I think we have to prepare for a marriage and a celebration the likes of which this kingdom has never seen!"

And so began the rule of Prince Horatio and Princess Alia.

Note: This story was inspired by the German fairy tale, collected by The Brothers Grimm: *The Frog Prince, 1812.*

When a Star Falls

Once upon a time, a little girl looked up to the night sky and asked her grandpa, "Dada, why are there so many stars in the sky?"

Her Dada looked down at her and said, "They are there—all of them—to celebrate all the children whom we have not taken care of."

"Not taken care of the children? What do you mean Dada?"

"Sometimes children are not taken care of by parents. Sometimes other members of the family abuse them."

"You mean parents and family are bad?"

"Bad is too strong a word, little one. Sometimes, when they themselves have not had enough love, they lose their way, and the children get hurt. Sometimes children get used in war as soldiers; sometimes their hospitals are bombed; sometimes children are used by their families to pay off family debts working in mines and factories: they do not get enough oxygen, and their lungs get sick, and they die; sometimes they drown as refugees with their families; sometimes they suffer and die from starvation in far off lands . . ."

"Dada, you must love me a lot, because I am not one of those children."

"Yes. You are our life. We love you and will always take care of you, and support you."

"Why do people hurt children? Why do they not take care of them, Dada?"

"It is like a circle, child. These adults have grown up not being loved, and so they have lost trust, and their hearts have shut down—they no longer care for anyone else, not even themselves."

"Dada, when I grow up, I'll make sure that my heart never shuts down. I will find a way to take care of those children."

"Yes, my child. We shall fill you with all the love you'll need . . . and you will be like a lamp in the dark places of life. You will always have my blessings, little one."

"Dada, when I save a child, what happens to the stars?"

"Every time you save a little one, a star will shoot across the sky! We call that a falling star. When you see one, get down on your knees and give thanks, for someone has saved a child!"

To this day, whenever Nokomis sees a star shoot across the evening skies, she bends her knees in thanks, and remembers her grandfather, Mahaway.

Note: This story was inspired by *The Song of Hiawatha, 1855,* by Henry Wadsworth Longfellow.

Jack and Mom Up the Beanstalk

It was some years after Jack first went up the beanstalk. That first time, he had grabbed the bag of gold. He and his mom had lived merrily off the gold. They never thought of saving a penny for a rainy day, or of investing for the future.

Well, one fine day, they ran out of food, and Jack's thoughts drifted back to the giant who lived at the top of the beanstalk. What if he were to go back there? Finally, Jack discussed it with his mom.

"What if you never came back?" she hollered at him. "You were lucky that first time because his wife trusted you. It won't be that easy the second time around. Why don't you let me go up with you?"

"Mom, you cannot climb that beanstalk, and I do not know if it could take the weight of us both!"

"Don't you worry Jack. You go up first, and when you are nearing the top, take this apple and drop it down. I'll begin to climb. Go slowly and wait for me."

The very next morning, before the sun was up, they put their plan into effect. All went well. It took Jack fifteen minutes to climb to the top. He dropped the apple and waited. Mom arrived in another twenty minutes. Mom had filled her pockets with dried fruit and nuts, and as they walked, they munched. They walked it seemed for miles and miles, but there was no cottage and no giant. Instead, there were lush fields of farmers working. Children and parents were busy weeding and planting the land.

There were huge bins of seeds of every variety, and people were helping themselves to these seeds. Further away, there were large, flat trays. People were lugging bags and emptying them onto these trays.

Jack politely asked—for he was new in town—what were they doing.

"We are bringing back seeds. We always save the seeds when we use the fruit. We bring them here to dry them out, and then they are sorted and go into the large bins. Anyone can help themselves."

"You mean you can just take them? You don't have to pay for them?"

"No, no, no! We no longer use money. That is so passé! We give freely, and we take freely. We take only what we need . . . because it will always be there for us."

Jack and his mom walked through the fields and were invited to help themselves to the produce.

As the evening drew to a close, a young couple invited them to spend the night with them. "Tomorrow, if you wish to stay with us, we'll gather together and build you a cottage. You'll have your own place, and you can stay with us for as long as you wish. Everyone can plant in the fields. That's how we live. If you have too much, you can exchange with others."

It was so wonderful. It was the end of worry about food, about money, about not having friends who cared.

Jack and his mother never returned down the beanstalk. The people who lived down below found their bodies frozen in their beds. They had passed away from starvation and cold.

Note: This story was inspired by *Jack and The Beanstalk*, an English fairy tale, told in 1734 as *The Story of Jack Spriggins and the Enchanted Bean.*

Acknowledgements

I am beholden to the passionate beta group of the creative writing class-*Write Impressions*-at the Active Adult Centre in Mississauga, whose support, commentary, and camaraderie were indispensable along this journey.

To my colleagues Ramabai Espinet and Clara Mohammed, for their professional support and guidance along my journey as a writer, and in particular, in concluding this work.

To Sophie Robov, I owe a debt of gratitude for her very timely responses to my need for a second pair of eyes, for professional expertise in accessing information, and a wealth of experience in editing. She has been my "right-hand man" when I've been under pressure.

To my very large family, but especially to Moreena, Shameen, Anya, David, and Sophie; to friends Clara, Horace, Jane, and others, for their understanding and support during these tough years of Covid-19, when all support systems were mostly virtual: they never gave up on me, and the writing of this book.

Lightning Source UK Ltd.
Milton Keynes UK
UKRC031208281022
411253UK00001B/3